THE ROYAL WEDDING CRASHERS

Clémentine Beauvais

Illustrated by Becka Moor

BLOOMSBURY

LONDON NEW DELHI NEW YORK SYDNEY

Bloomsbury Publishing, London, New Delhi, New York and Sydney

First published in Great Britain in May 2015 by Bloomsbury Publishing Plc
50 Bedford Square, London WC1B 3DP

www.bloomsbury.com

Bloomsbury is a registered trademark of Bloomsbury Publishing Plc

A CIP catalogue record for this book is available from the British Library

ISBN 978 1 4088 5544 7

FSC
www.fsc.org
MIX
Paper from
responsible sources
FSC® C020471

Printed and bound in Great Britain
by CPI Group (UK) Ltd, Croydon CR0 4YY

1 3 5 7 9 10 8 6 4 2

The story so far …

BRITLAND BLATHER

'PRINCE PEPINO NOT COMPLETELY USELESS AFTER ALL,' KING AND QUEEN DECLARE

After eight and three-quarter years of being unremarkable, Prince Pepino almost-single-handedly repelled an invasion, yesterday.

'We are pleased to inform the people of Britland that, without Prince Pepino, they would all have been turned into slaves or meatballs by King Alaspooryorick of Daneland yesterday,' the King told our Royal reporter. 'The invader's attack was fought off by Prince Pepino, his six little brothers and two local girls. They used cheeses, catapults and snotty handkerchiefs.' The Queen and the King were not able to help, since they were on their

annual day of holiday in the Independent Republic of Slough, where they were spotted squirting rather a lot of mayonnaise on their chocolate sundaes.

The 'two local girls' have been identified as sisters Holly and Anna Burnbright, who were Royal-Babysitting for the day. It is rumoured that Prince Pepino might now be friends with the young ladies. Prince Pepino was unavailable for comment, since his mouth was full of caramel fudge. Anna Burnbright stated: 'Yes, we saved the country. You're welcome. But sorry, we need to go now; yesterday's job didn't earn us any money, so we have to find another one. We want to buy tickets to an amazing Holy Moly Holiday, you see.'

Chapter One

Big fluffy spiders make better pets than puppies: they've got more eyes, and they're better at knitting. Like most puppies, they enjoy nibbling at people just for fun; however, unlike most puppies, their bites are generally venomous. This is why Prince Pepino, who had just received a big fluffy pet tarantula as a present from his godfather the Tsar of Marok, was now covered

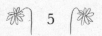

in greenish poisonous spider bites from the tip of his nose to his big toe.

'She's doing it *again*! Ouch! Stop it, Charlotte A. Rainier, you bloodthirsty terrorist!'

Charlotte A. Rainier – the tarantula – couldn't help it: Prince Pepino's right little finger was just too appealing. It was perfectly plump, and smelt of cactus ice cream. She knew it wasn't nice of her, but she had to – SNAP! – bite it.

'That's it! That's it!' Pepino shouted. 'I'm going to – flatten – you – like a – pancake!'

He tried, but Charlotte A. Rainier was faster.

'Pepino, how *dare* you!' scolded Holly
Burnbright, picking up Charlotte A. Rainier
from the floor to stroke her.

'She *bit* me!' Pepino retorted. 'She bites me all
the time!'

'She's just playing,' said Holly. 'Look at her sorry little eyes, all eight of them. She didn't mean any harm.'

And Holly looked lovingly at Charlotte, who had quickly woven herself a little hammock between her fingers, and was now having a nap and snoring.

'Ahem!' coughed Nestor. 'I thought you three were interested in finding a summer job.'

Indeed they were. Prince Pepino of Britland and his friends, Holly and Anna, were in urgent need of one thousand five hundred pounds. *Urgent*, that is, because Anna would not give up her dream of going on a Holy Moly Holiday she had seen advertised in the newspaper. And Pepino and Holly knew better than to argue with her.

Plus, the Holy Moly Holiday did sound *extremely cool*.

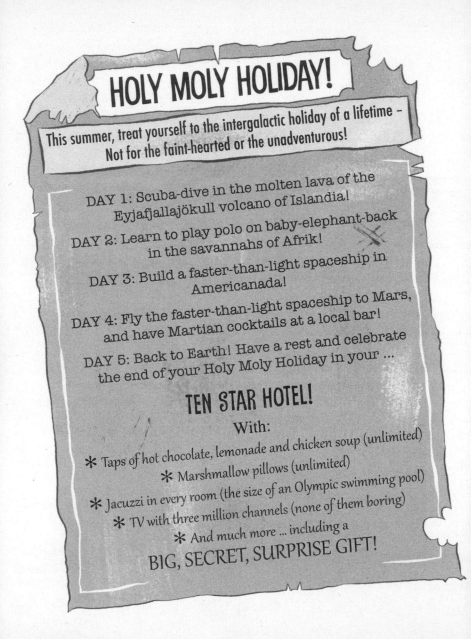

'There's a flower-planting job here,' said Nestor.

WWF

FLOWER-PLANTING IN ARKTIK

Successful candidates will spend eight days planting flowers on the Arktik ice cap to give seals and penguins something pretty to look at!

'Oh, that would be wonderful!' Holly said. 'I love penguins!'

'Sounds awful,' Anna said. 'How much do they pay?'

'You get a penguin-shaped key ring with your name stamped on it,' replied Nestor.

'Scam!' Anna snorted. 'Give us a *real* job.'

'Well,' said Nestor, 'The King and Queen of Britland need babysitters for their toddlers; their annual day of leave went so well that they've decided to take a whole week of holiday ...'

'*That,*' said Anna, 'is out of the question.

We did one day of Royal-Babysitting, Nestor, remember? And it was *hell*.'

'Not to mention, again, *unpaid*,' said Holly politely. 'Aren't there any jobs that would pay us some *money*?'

Just then, the door of the Doverport Job Agency opened with a *ding!* The person who walked in was quite a sight.

Even Charlotte A. Rainier couldn't help staring at her.

'C-c-can I help?' stuttered Nestor eventually.

'Certainly,' said the young lady in a faint Francian accent. 'My name is Mademoiselle Malypense, and this is my dog, Kiki-Bisou. I am looking for a young Britlander to help me with a difficult sort of task.'

'W-w-w-what kind of t-t-t-ask?' asked Nestor.

'In two days, Princess Violette of Francia is getting married to King Dentu of Romany. As Princess Violette's closest friend, I'm in charge of the Royal Wedding. And I need someone to run a few errands for me in Parii, the capital of Francia.'

'Parii!' Holly whispered dreamily.

'W-w-hat k-kind of errands?' Nestor asked.

'Oh, nothing too difficult,' said Mademoiselle Malypense. 'But it's *confidential*. I can't employ a Francian because Francian people can't keep secrets. I'm looking for someone who can.'

'Pick me! Pick me!!' said Pepino. 'I've never told anyone else's secrets!'

'That's because no one's ever told you any secrets,' Anna smirked.

'That's not true! Holly told me how you still can't fall asleep without sucking your th–'

'Pepino's right,' Holly interrupted, 'Maybe *we* could work for you, Mademoiselle Malypense! Two days ago we babysat six royal toddlers and repelled an invasion at the same time! Now we're totally used to royal families, and keeping secrets about their bad habits.'

'Really?' said Mademoiselle Malypense. She went up to Nestor's desk. 'Are these children any good?'

'C-c-certainly,' Nestor stuttered. 'I helped repel the invasion too. I threw cheeses at robotic mermaids.'

'Did you *really*?' chimed Mademoiselle Malypense. 'What a *hero*.'

Being called a hero by a young Francian lady was too much for Nestor: he fainted away behind his desk.

'So?' Holly asked. 'Will you hire us?'

'Yes,' said Mademoiselle Malypense. 'Follow me.'

'Holly, what are you *doing*? You haven't even asked *me* what I think about all this,' Anna said. 'We don't need to go to Parii. We need to find a well-paid job quick, and go on the Holy Moly Holiday!'

'But a trip to Francia!' Holly piped up. 'That's almost as good as a Holy Moly Holiday!'

Anna folded her arms. 'I am not going to help organise some silly princess's wedding. I'm

done with royalty! They're all nuts. And I hate weddings! They're for soppy, lovey-dovey idiots. I want to go volcano-scuba-diving!'

'You'd get paid twenty francs,' said Mademoiselle Malypense.

'That's terrible,' Anna grumbled.

'Twenty Francian francs,' said Mademoiselle Malypense coldly, 'are worth a thousand Britland pounds. *Each*.'

When Nestor woke up and emerged from behind his desk, the Doverport Job Agency was empty.

'Prince Pepino? Anna? Holly? Where are you?'

He ran out into the street, and looked out to the wide Francian Channel Sea – just in time to catch a last glimpse of the boat that was taking them away to Francia.

Chapter Two

They had a healthy picnic on the boat: snail lollipops, frogs' legs sandwiches, baguettes, and very strong coffee served in thimbles. The coffee made Prince Pepino jumpy and he fell out of the boat eleven times. In the end, the girls fastened his foot to a solid thread woven by Charlotte A. Rainier, and it was easy to fish him out again after that.

At dusk, the Royal Boat began to worm its way up the long and windy river which led to Parii. They got there at midnight. The city was beautiful under the light of the croissant moon.

'Wow!' Pepino marvelled. 'When I become King, the first thing I do will be to invade this place and make it *mine*!'

'What a silly little prince,' sniggered Mademoiselle Malypense. 'You wouldn't last a week.'

'Pepino isn't a silly little prince!' said Holly indignantly.

'Well, he is *sometimes*,' Anna rectified.

'OK, he is *often*,' said Holly.

'Whatever you are, you would do well to hide your princely status here, Your Little Majesty,' stated Mademoiselle Malypense as they drifted past the riverbanks. 'Francian people are not fond of royalty.'

'They'll be fond of *me*,' Pepino assured her. 'I'll make every Friday National Ice-Cream Day. And all the other days *International* Ice-Cream Days.'

But even though the crown on Pepino's head was covered in seaweed, it did seem to be attracting strange glances from the people of Parii. And when they got off the boat, a welcoming committee was waiting to greet them.

'Good evening, Mademoiselle!' chimed the
Pariisian Beheader. 'Is that a prince you've got
there?'

'We won't be needing your services, thank you
very much,' said Mademoiselle Malypense.

'Just one little cut and the job's done! No

more nasty head on those lovely shoulders –
guaranteed without pain!'

'I said *no thank you*. This boy is not royalty.
He's simply amusing himself with a plastic
crown.'

'Hey!' Pepino burst out. 'Those are real
diam–'

'Shut up, Pepino!' said Anna, slamming her
hand over Pepino's mouth. 'From now on, you're
our little brother.'

'Your *big* brother,' grumbled Pepino.

'Nope, sorry – we have to keep it believable.'

And she threw Pepino's crown into the depths of the river.

'Good,' said Mademoiselle Malypense. 'Let's go to the Royal Palace. As soon as the sun rises, you'll start your special missions. I mean, your work.'

They began to walk through the dark streets of Parii. Pepino trotted right behind Mademoiselle Malypense, his hands on his head.

'This is horrible!' he moaned. 'It's like I've lost half of my head! I've never *ever* not had my crown!'

'Surely you take it off to go to bed?' said Mademoiselle Malypense.

'Never! What if I had dreams where I wasn't a prince?'

While Pepino and Mademoiselle Malypense were talking, Anna elbowed her sister a few times ('Ouch!' 'Ouch!' 'Ouch!') until she slowed down.

'Holly, why would she ask Britlanders to help with the Francian Royal Wedding?'

'She said we were better at keeping secrets,' said Holly. 'She said she's the princess's best friend. She's probably got lots of fun things

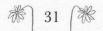

planned, and wants to keep them a surprise.'

'It's weird,' said Anna. 'I smell a rat.'

'That's because there's one just under your nose,' replied Holly.

'Yuck!'

'Seriously, Anna, we'll be fine. This is a great job, in the most beautiful city in the world!'

'Really? Beautiful? How about *that*?'

That was a large and spiky-looking palace at the heart of the city. Mademoiselle Malypense was leading them straight to it.

'Are you expecting an invasion?' Pepino asked.

'Always,' said Mademoiselle Malypense as they walked through the super-protected courtyard. 'But you'll be safe here.'

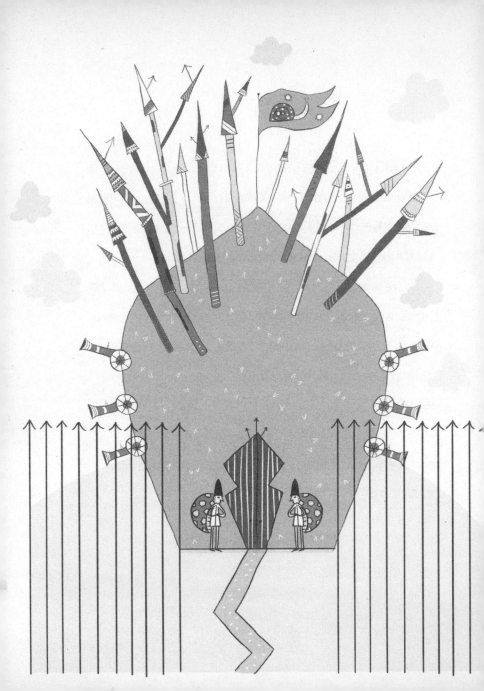

'Will we?' Anna asked. 'Why do your guards have such big suits of armour?'

'The last ones weren't thick enough,' replied Mademoiselle Malypense elusively.

'Thick enough for what?' asked Pepino. 'Oh, look! That painting's got a hole in it. Even two. Three … Four!'

'Yes, the artwork keeps getting damaged,' sighed Mademoiselle Malypense. 'Oh, a boomerang – duck!'

Everyone dived to the floor as a flying croissant came crashing through a window, twirled in the air above their heads and left again by the hole it had made.

'Does that happen often?' Holly asked with some nervousness.

'Oh, you'll smell them coming after a while. That lovely, buttery, deathly smell.'

Mademoiselle Malypense rushed them
through the corridor and opened a door. 'Here's
your room. The bathroom is next door. I live just
above, if you need me.'

'Who do you think might invade the
palace?' asked Anna. 'King Alaspooryorick of
Daneland?'

'Oh, no. Just Pariisians. But you don't need to

worry about it. Not tonight, at least.'

'When will we need to worry, then?' Anna asked defiantly.

'Probably tomorrow,' said Mademoiselle Malypense. 'I hear they're planning another riot.'

Chapter Three

The next morning, the rising sun ate up the croissant moon, leaving crumbs everywhere for the pigeons to eat.

Mademoiselle Malypense marched into their room. 'Good morning, children. I have a mission for you. In fact, three missions.'

She opened a curtain to reveal a large portrait.

'This is the Francian Royal Family.'

'Their heads aren't quite right,' Pepino observed.

'I assure you they are quite normal,' Mademoiselle Malypense replied. 'Like all Francian royalty, King Louis the Eighty-Ninth and Queen Marianne were beheaded when they took the throne. Now they carry their heads around in fashionable handbags. And these are their daughters, Princess Violette and Princess Bella.'

'Princess Violette is beautiful!' Holly said.

Mademoiselle Malypense coughed. 'Well,' she said, 'she isn't *too* ugly, I guess. I don't notice it at all, of course, since I've known her all my life. We were brought up together, you see: my mother was the palace cook. As a result, Violette and I are very good friends.' She coughed again.

'Now, here's a picture of King Dentu of Romany.'

'Urgh,' said Anna.

'Erm,' said Holly.

'Wow,' said Pepino, 'he looks a bit –'

'That's quite enough chit-chat,' said Mademoiselle Malypense. 'As you know, I am organising their wedding, and I'm missing three *very* important things. I would like *you* to get them for me. You will have three days. Here's the Mission Plan for Day One. Get started *now*.'

She handed the rolled-up piece of paper, tied with blue ribbon, to Anna, and turned around. 'Good luck! And … be careful.'

She left the room, and Anna, Pepino and Holly read their mission.

'Seems straightforward enough,' said Anna.

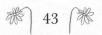

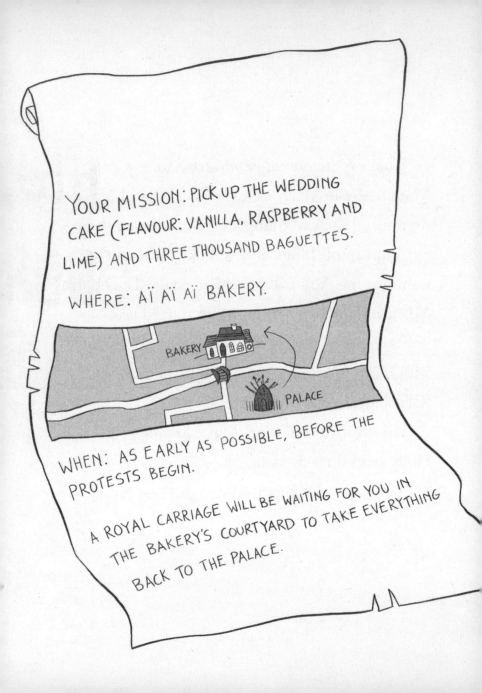

'Let's go!'

'Wait, I'll get my camera,' said Pepino. 'I want to show Mum and Dad how pretty it is here. Maybe they'll buy me Francia for my birthday.'

'You're not on holiday, you know, Pepino. You're not here to take pictures. You're here to *work*.'

But Pepino tucked his camera in his inside pocket, as well as a telescopic stand.

'OK,' said Holly as they left the Royal Palace. 'We have to cross that bridge over there. Easy.'

'I'm not sure "easy" is the right word,' Anna

mumbled. 'It looks ... *busy*.'

The bridge was swarming with people screaming things in Francian. It wasn't clear whether they were extremely happy or scarily angry, but at least a few were kissing while others were fighting in a corner.

'That might be just what Francia is like,' said Holly as they squeezed through. 'We need to be respectful of other countries.'

'Especially the ones I'll invade when I'm a grown-up king,' said Pepino.

'Shush, Pepino! They'll chop your head off if

they hear you!'

Crawling under legs and armpits, they reached the other side of the bridge. Pepino turned around. 'It seems to be some kind of meeting,' said the prince. 'About *pain*.'

'Pain? What pain?'

'I don't know. Maybe they're the Francian Society for Pain.'

He pointed to a group of Francian protesters carrying banners saying *PAIN!* and *ON VEUT DU PAIN!*

'What on earth does that mean?' Holly said.

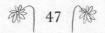

'Who cares,' replied Anna. 'Maybe they just love pain. Let's go – we're looking for a little street on the left ...'

They began to walk, but suddenly they heard a noise behind them.

Just a faint noise at first, like a rhinoceros grumbling.

But then it grew to the noise of a rhinoceros *charging*.

And then they realised it wasn't a rhinoceros at all. It was THREE of them.

'CHARRRRRRGE!!!!!!!!'

'It looks like the police,' said Holly. 'How interesting things are here in Fran–'

'Holly – RUN!'

Anna grabbed her sister by a plait and Pepino
by the tip of his seaweed scarf, and they
whooshed back the way they'd come …

… where they met the protesters they'd just
left on the bridge. They were now marching up

the avenue, *towards* the rhinoceroses.

'Oh *great*,' Anna cursed. 'We're trapped.'

'Wow, super exciting! I need to take a picture of this!' said Pepino.

But as soon as he'd set up the camera, the

protesters and rhinoceros police stopped in their tracks and posed.

They coughed, tut-tutted, and readjusted their hats and banners, twirling around to give Pepino their best profiles.

Flash! Flash! Flash!

'Say CHEESE!' Pepino
mouthed to a sulky protester,
taking his 783rd photo.

'*Cheese.*'

A murmur went
through the crowd.

'Cheese?'

'*Cheese.*'

'We cannot 'ave
cheese,' shouted a
protester, 'wizout BREAD!'

'Yes, bread! *DU PAIN! DU PAIN!*' screamed everyone else, and they waved their banners with '*Pain*' written all over them.

'Oh, I get it,' Holly said. 'That word *pain* means *bread*. They want bread. That makes more sense than wanting pain.'

'Yes, we want bread! We are starving without bread!' the woman next to them explained, 'and meanwhile, the Royal Family is having a wedding with three thousand baguettes! *Three thousand!* There are none left for us!'

'Oh, that's terrible of them,' Anna said.

'Royal families really are royally selfish.'

'Hey!' Pepino objected.

'Yes!' said the lady. 'That's why we're here today: to catch the people who are supposed to be picking up the three thousand baguettes. We know they are getting them from Aï Aï Aï Bakery, and we'll stop them!'

'Not if we *stop you* first!' the chief policeman on his rhinoceros shouted. 'CHAAAARGE!'

'*DU PAIN!*' the crowd shouted.

And they galloped towards each other ...

'Charging rhinoceroses!' screamed Pepino.

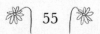

'I need to take a picture of *that*!'

   He straightened his camera stand …

   And at the last second …

   The ground under their feet …

   Collapsed!

Chapter Four

A minute later, the three children were riding large rats at great speed through the sewers of Parii.

'Pepino,' said Holly, 'that was a brilliant idea.'

'Oh, I suppose you could say that,' said Pepino, glowing red.

'It wasn't exactly his *idea*,' said Anna. 'If his camera stand hadn't pulled the cover off that manhole, we'd never have fallen into it.'

'Well,' said Pepino, 'at least my *camera stand* has good ideas.'

'Jump down, everyone!' Anna said. 'We're here – right underneath the bakery.'

'How do you know?' asked Holly.

'Well,' Anna replied, 'there's a terrified-looking baker right there.'

'*Bonjour!*' said Anna, and the cloud of flour made her sneeze: '*Achoo!*'

'*Atchoum!*' the man sneezed too (for '*atchoum*' is the Francian way of sneezing).

'What – are – you – doing – 'ere?' asked Anna very slowly and in a Francian accent.

The man replied with a perfect Britland Broadcast Company accent. 'I'm hiding from the crazy mob. They want to burn my shop and steal my bread. I was up – *Atchoum!* – all night baking three thousand baguettes and a wedding cake for the Royal Wedding, but no one's come to collect them. And now I'm in huge – *Atchoum!* – trouble.'

'Well,' said Pepino, 'you're in luck! It's us. We've come to collect the three thousand baguettes and the wedding cake.'

The baker jumped up. 'Oh, thank goodness! Come up – quick!'

He led them down a low corridor, then up a floury ladder and through a trapdoor into his bakery.

It would have been a nice bakery, if there hadn't been dozens of Pariisians climbing

through the broken windows, upsetting the pyramids of colourful macaron biscuits, the steamy croissants and the delicate chocolate éclairs in their search for bread!

'Quick,' said the baker, 'this way!'

He took them to the back of the shop, where three big tin boxes and a beautiful wedding cake were waiting.

'Nice cake,' said Pepino appreciatively. 'And the little figures at the top look just like Princess Violette and King Dentu!'

'How are you taking them back to the palace?'

'There's supposed to be a royal carriage waiting for us.'

'Oh,' said the baker, 'you mean that one?'

'Pariisians like to, erm, burn carriages,' he said sadly. 'They're funny like that.

Maybe the police will take you to the palace instead?'

Holly looked back into the shop: two scared police rhinoceroses had just smashed through the shop window and were now grazing on strawberry tartlets. It didn't look as if the police

were still around to offer protection.

'We need to go back through the sewers,' said Anna. 'That's the only way. These tin boxes are light enough to float – we can use them as boats.'

The crowd was invading the shop, screaming, '*DU PAIN! DU PAIN!*'

'I'm not going back there,' said Pepino. 'It doesn't smell nice.'

'*You* don't smell nice,' Anna observed. 'That seaweed scarf stinks! Hurry up!'

First they lowered the big boxes down to the mucky, dirty, dark water.

'And now, the wedding cake,' said the baker. 'Careful! I spent a long time on that.'

'That cream looks sooooo yummy,' said Pepino, salivating.

'Don't touch it!' the baker warned. 'It's not for you.'

'I know, I'm not a baby,' Pepino grumbled, but as soon as the baker had turned around, he dipped his fingers in the icing, and …

They carried the wedding cake through the shop. The deafening mob and the two rhinoceroses had destroyed almost everything.

'The poor people of Parii,' said Holly to her sister. 'Can you imagine having no bread to go with your cheese?'

'I can think of worse things,' said Anna. 'Like not having a Holy Moly Holiday.'

But Holly had spotted shelves behind her, covered with appetising loaves and marked BRIOCHE.

'*Brioche!* I'm not sure what it is, but it looks a bit like bread, doesn't it? It must be almost as good.'

And cupping her hands around her lips, she screamed, 'PEOPLE OF PARII! IF YOU CAN'T HAVE BREAD, WHY NOT TRY BRIOCHE?'

Everyone stopped – even the rhinoceroses, who were covered in custard from the tartlets.

'Why not indeed!' said Anna. 'Quick, Holly, come down before they all –'

Holly jumped through the trapdoor just in time – a fraction of a second later, the stampede above their heads indicated that the happy crowd was rushing towards the cupboard of brioche.

'You've got a cheek!' the baker complained. 'I'd baked that for the anniversary of the King's beheading, next week!'

But the three children had already jumped on the boxes of baguettes and were sailing down the sewer, Holly holding tightly to the beautiful wedding cake.

'Where does this tunnel lead?' asked Holly.

'Probably to the river,' Anna replied.

She was right: it did lead to the river.

Unfortunately, she hadn't anticipated exactly

how far down the river would be from the sewers …

'Everyone alive?' asked Pepino.

'More importantly, is the *cake* alive?' asked Anna.

'Yes,' said Holly in a slightly offended voice. 'I'm glad to hear you care more about the cake than *me*.'

'I'll care about you all you like when we're on the Holy Moly Holiday. Now row – we have to cross the river!'

'We don't have any oars, sails or engines,' remarked Pepino, 'nor any servants to do it for us.'

'Then paddle with your hands, lazybones!'

As soon as they reached the other side, they dragged the wet boxes on to the bank – and breathed out.

'Now back to the Palace,' Holly said. 'Then we can prepare for the next mission.'

Pepino looked at the watch he'd drawn in felt tips on his wrist, but it had been almost entirely erased by all his recent encounters with water.

'Can we have ice cream first?' he asked. 'Surely it's ice-cream time!'

'It's not,' said Anna. 'It's bring-the-wedding-cake-to-Mademoiselle-Malypense-time.'

'But I *need* ice cream! I have a bad taste in my mouth,' Pepino said.

'You probably swallowed something from the sewers,' said Holly. 'I don't want to know what.'

'No,' Pepino shook his head. 'It's the *cake*. I ate a bit of cream from the top. It was DISGUSTING.'

'Really? That's strange. It looks delicious.'

'It's AWFUL,' said Pepino. 'If my Royal Baker produced a cake like that, I'd have him baked into Dorsettish Pasties.'

Anna and Holly exchanged a glance.

'You go first,' said Anna.

'No, after you,' said Holly politely.

'Both together, then,' Anna offered.

So, at the same time, they scraped a bit of the creamy icing at the top of the wedding cake, and licked their fingers.

'YUCK!'

'URGH!'

'Told you!' said Pepino.

'It tastes of ...'

'There's definitely ...'

'I *told* you!'

'... *Garlic* in there!'

'How weird,' Anna observed. 'The Mission Plan said the cake was vanilla, raspberry and lime. Do you think it's normal, in Francia, to have garlic icing on a wedding cake? Maybe it's so normal that they don't even bother mentioning it?'

'Maybe,' Holly whispered. 'Or maybe not ...'

Chapter Five

Back at the palace, Mademoiselle Malypense patted their heads lightly, and then wiped her hand several times on a silk tea towel.

'Well done, children. Even though you did ride those boxes of bread through the sewers of Parii, at least the baguettes didn't get wet.'

'Just one little thing, though,' said Anna. 'We think there might have been a mistake at the bakery. The Royal Wedding Cake has garlic icing on it.'

'And it's *disgusting*,' Pepino added pointedly. 'Not at all fit for a Royal Wedding. If I married someone, like you, for instance, I wouldn't want a garlicky wedding cake.'

Mademoiselle Malypense grew slightly paler than the icing on the cake. 'You *tasted* the Royal Wedding Cake?'

'Oh *no*,' said Anna 'not even slightly, at all, but … erm …'

'We noticed that the baker had been using

garlic cream,' Holly interrupted. 'There was a whole empty tube of it in his kitchen.'

'He must have been using it for something else,' said Mademoiselle Malypense coolly. 'I don't pay you to be concerned about such things. Just get me what I *need*. Read the Mission Plan for your next instructions.'

She turned around, and Kiki-Bisou turned at the same time, his little paws clicking on the floor. 'And *please*,' said Mademoiselle Malypense, 'have a *shower*!'

Anna squeezed the quite-wet, quite-smelly
Top Secret Mission Plan out of her pocket.
The page now read:

MISSION ONE...
ACCOMPLISHED!

THIS MISSION PLAN WILL BE
DESTROYED

IN TEN SECONDS

NINE -
EIGHT-
SEVEN-

Anna dropped the plan.

Six seconds later, a trapdoor opened in the floor and a suspicious-looking rat, wearing a balaclava and gloves, scuttled into the room.

After he had chewed every last bit of the plan, he scuttled away again, leaving behind him a new rolled-up piece of paper tied with white ribbon.

'All right,' said Anna. 'What's our second mission, then?'

Pepino unrolled the scroll:

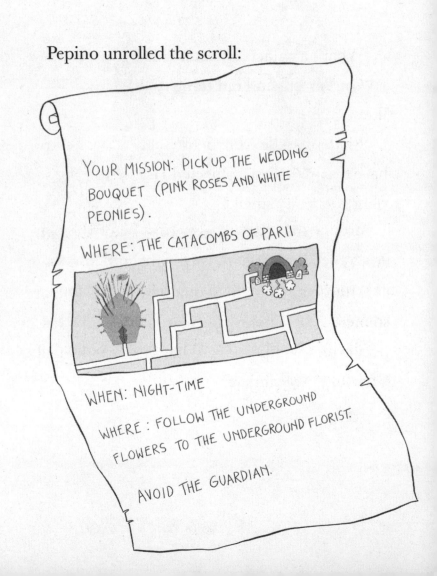

YOUR MISSION: PICK UP THE WEDDING BOUQUET (PINK ROSES AND WHITE PEONIES).

WHERE: THE CATACOMBS OF PARII

WHEN: NIGHT-TIME

WHERE : FOLLOW THE UNDERGROUND FLOWERS TO THE UNDERGROUND FLORIST.

AVOID THE GUARDIAN.

'What's a catacomb?' asked Holly.

'Guess we'll find out tonight,' said Anna. 'Let's go!'

'Mademoiselle Malypense said we'd need to have a shower first,' objected Holly. 'And she's right: we really smell.'

'That's true. Well, Pepino in particular,' said Anna.

'I absolutely don't,' Pepino protested. 'You are so mean.' He squeezed his tarantula out of his pocket and whispered into her face, 'Do I smell, Charlotte A. Rainier?'

 85

'Shower time!' Anna shouted.

'I don't have *showers*,' Pepino sniffed. 'I have bubble baths. And then only in my swimming-pool-sized bright blue bathtub.'

He curled up in a corner and sulked. Meanwhile, Holly and Anna showered in the next-door bathroom.

Then they pounced on Pepino: Charlotte tied his hands behind his head with ultra-strong thread, Anna and Holly stripped him down to his flowery underpants, and they pushed him into the shower. He refused point-blank to let go of his seaweed scarf. Three or four small crabs crawled out of it and scampered away.

'*That* was what was prickling my neck!'

PSHHHH!

'*Grrbbllb!* You're drowning me! How dare you – *kof!* – do that to a prince of the crown of Britland!'

'Anna,' said Holly, who was holding the shower head, 'stop singing and make sure you rub that shampoo into Pepino's hair.'

'I'm not singing!' Anna replied, creating a mass of soap suds. 'You are!'

'No, I'm not! Is it you, Pepino?'

'I'm not – *kof!* – singing! I'm drowning!'

'Well, who's singing, then?'

Holly turned off the water. 'Ex*cuse* me,' said Pepino. '*Hello?* How am I supposed to get the soap out without water?'

But Holly wasn't interested. She could hear some singing, echoing through the pipes.

'It must be coming from the kitchen upstairs,' Holly muttered. 'We're just a floor down from Mademoiselle Malypense's apartments ...'

Then they heard whistling, and then profound sighing ... and then Mademoiselle Malypense's voice!

'Oh!' sighed Mademoiselle Malypense. 'It *is* love ... How to explain it otherwise? ... Tra-lalala-lalala ... *mon amouuuuur*... I can't stop thinking of that face!'

'Do you think she's talking about me?' Pepino asked.

Mademoiselle Malypense's voice resonated again. 'But *he* is *royalty*! And I'm a *nobody*! Oh, how unfair ...'

'It doesn't matter!' Pepino whispered. 'We can still be happy together! I'll go tell her –'

'But if this plan works, there is still *hope* ... Oh, am I doing the right thing, Kiki-Bisou?' asked Mademoiselle Malypense. 'I am taking insane risks. But to think

that he is
marrying *her*!
A man like *him*!'

And she began to
sing again, a song in Francian,
probably about love and suffering.

'Oh,' Pepino sighed. 'Not me, then.'

'Don't worry, Pepino,' said Holly
sympathetically, starting the water again with a
SSHLPPHHH! 'In a few years' time, I'm sure all
the Francian ladies will fall in love with you and
sing to their dogs about it.'

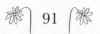

'But not this one,' smiled Anna. 'How interesting ... Mademoiselle Malypense must be in love with King Dentu!'

'Which is *why* she's trying to ruin his wedding to Princess Violette,' Holly chuckled. 'By giving them a disgusting wedding cake!'

'Most rubbish strategy I've ever heard,' Anna pondered. 'Why would King Dentu be so upset about the cake that he'd call the whole wedding off?'

'I would!' Pepino piped from inside the shower.

'I bet you would,' Anna smirked. 'Yes, I suppose royalty are often weird like that. Maybe Mademoiselle Malypense is hoping that he'll be so upset that he'll run away, and then she'll console him and he'll marry her.'

Holly laughed. 'That's the most bizarre plan *I've* ever heard. But what should we do about it? It's partly our fault – she's asking us to complete these missions in order to ruin the wedding. Do you think we should tell someone?'

'No!' Anna replied. 'It's a *job*. We'll finish it, get paid, and go on the Holy Moly Holiday.

I don't care about the love stories of Francian and Romanyi royalty. We'll just do what we're asked.'

She fished out the Mission Plan from her pocket, and unfolded it:

'And what we're asked to do right now is to get the Wedding Bouquet.'

Chapter Six

They reached the entrance to the Catacombs a little before midnight. It was just a door to what looked like a cupboard, with no other monument in sight. They pushed the door – and almost fell down a long, dark spiral staircase.

'What on earth is this place?' Anna whispered. 'It's like a stairway to hell!'

'Don't say that!' said Pepino, quivering. 'Why can't they be something else? I know – maybe

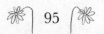

catacombs are the Francian word for a place where cats go to get their fur combed. Cat-a-comb!'

'No,' replied Holly. 'Anna's closer to the truth. Look – it says right *here* what catacombs are.'

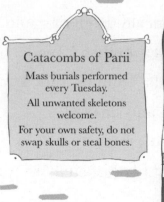

Catacombs of Parii

Mass burials performed every Tuesday.

All unwanted skeletons welcome.

For your own safety, do not swap skulls or steal bones.

'Ohhhh,' Pepino said, closing his eyes, 'I'll just pretend it says "Cat hairdresser".'

'You do that,' Anna sighed. 'Meanwhile, we're going down there.'

'Wait! Don't leave me alone here!'

They began to walk down the damp and dark spiral staircase, Pepino frantically muttering, 'This is a place where cats get combed.' Ten long minutes later they reached the bottom.

The air was humid, cold, and smelt of mushroom.

'Where are we going?' Anna whispered.

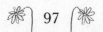

'Shall we ask this gentleman?' Holly suggested, pointing at someone in the distance.

'Doesn't look like a gentleman to me,' Anna murmured. 'More like a –'

'Cat hairdresser?' Pepino asked, full of hope.

'No. A GHOST! Quick – hide!'

The busy-looking ghost floated their way, wearing a milky-blue flat cap. He brushed past them but didn't notice them – and shimmered away into another corridor.

'That ghost is clearly the guardian of the Catacombs,' Anna interrupted. 'I don't suppose we're actually *allowed* to be here, so let's stay discreet. We need to find …'

'Oh, look, flowers!' Pepino piped. 'They've really made an effort to decorate these corridors.'

'Where?'

Pepino pointed at a trail of little daisies on the ground. They looked a bit sickly, barely had any petals left, and all of them were nibbled by insects, but they shimmered calmly in the dark.

'Great,' said Anna. 'The trail to the underground florist. Come on – let's *go*!'

And she ran away, following the wilting daisies
on the floor. Holly and Pepino trotted after her,
all the way to a chamber full of …

BONES!

'Oh I don't LIKE this!' Pepino cried. 'I'd
rather fight Alaspooryorick another time than
those!'

'They don't want to fight us,' Holly said
soothingly. 'They couldn't be quieter if they
tried. Come on, Pepino – pull yourself together.'

'Wait – I've lost Charlotte A. Rainier! She isn't
in my pocket any more!'

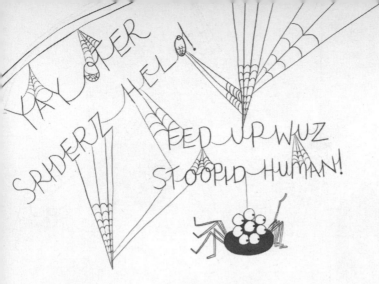

YAY OVER
SPIDERZ HELO!
FED UP WUZ
STOOPID HUMAN!

'She must be wandering around. She'll catch up.'

'No! What if she gets lost? Charlotte! Charlotte!'

Charlotte A. Rainier, in fact, was hanging from the arched ceiling having all the spidery fun in the world. She'd found dozens of new friends.

But Pepino, in the dark, was fumbling among the skeletons.

'Charlotte? Charlotte!'

'Pepino, we have to go!'

'Wait – I think I've just seen her ...'

BROOOOF!

In a cloud of dust, a pile of skeletons collapsed

under Pepino's weight. Twenty or so mice whooshed out.

'Oh, whoops,' said Pepino. 'Erm … just pretend you didn't see that. Look, it's fixed!'

He picked up a skull, placed it back on a body, and reattached a few arms and legs. 'I *think* that went there, and that one is supposed to go here …'

'Pepino,' Anna sighed, 'did you ever do jigsaw puzzles when you were a toddler?'

'Of course not!' Pepino replied. 'Princes have no time for jigsaw puzzles. As a toddler, I was

already fencing! With sharp carrots instead of swords, of course.'

'I *thought* so,' said Anna. 'I think you might have got it all a *bit* wrong.'

Clearly Anna wasn't the only one to think there was an issue.

The bearded baby skull's jaw fell open.

The dog's skull's jaw fell open.

The former boomed: 'What under Earth's happened to my *body*?'

The latter barked: '*WOOF!*'

And all the skeletons (well, those that still had skulls) *glared* at Holly, Anna and Pepino with their dark, empty, threatening eye sockets ...

'Pepino,' Holly sighed, 'remember how the board said, "for your own safety, do not swap skulls"?'

'Nope,' said Pepino. 'I chose to remember it as saying "Cat hairdresser".'

'Here we go again,' Anna said. 'Let's just leave discreetly ...'

But the big bearded skull on a baby skeleton's body followed them.

And so did a big dog skull on a big man's body.

As well as many other skeletons who'd been woken up, and were *very* interested to know what under Earth was going on.

Chapter Seven

'Oh dear,' Holly puffed, '*this* is what happens when you help evil people like Mademoiselle Malypense! I can't *believe* I wanted this job. It wouldn't have happened if we'd gone for that honest flower-planting job!'

'It's all right for you to say that *now*,' Anna replied. 'Who was it again who so wanted to see Parii? Uh-oh – here's another one …'

Clickety flocks of skeletons were trickling in. Thankfully, a lot of them were too sleepy to realise that they should have been chasing the three humans.

'Is this a party?' a very ancient-looking skeleton asked Holly. 'There hasn't been a party here since 1789!'

And he started dancing with a skull-less skeleton who was still wearing a big ragged dress.

The ones that weren't dancing, however, were ready to fight.

'Skull-swappers! You're done for!' the bearded baby bawled.

'*Woof!*' the man-dog added. And behind them, the rickety army nodded their skulls gravely.

'Can't we just be friends?' Pepino suggested.

'You've played jigsaw-puzzle with their bodies!' Anna shouted. 'I don't think they'll forgive you this easily. Come on, let's fight them off!'

She dived into a pile of old bones and drew out a few big ones – *very* big ones – that must have belonged to a tall animal. A big animal.

A tall, big, scary animal.

Anna was ready to face the skeleton army.

'Oh that is TOO unfair!' Pepino protested. 'Why don't *I* get to wear the T-Rex armour? I could tell all my mates at school when I'm back after the hols!'

'You have neither *mates* nor a *school*,' said Holly. 'And *hols* is a ridiculous word. Get your own weapons and *fight*!'

'Phew! That was close,' puffed Pepino. 'Can we keep the T-Rex costume?'

'If you can carry it,' said Anna, throwing it to him.

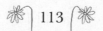

But Pepino collapsed under the weight of the skull and bones, so he had to bid it farewell. Thankfully, he was soon distracted by the sight of another daisy.

'And another one! And another one!'

From chamber to chamber they ran, picking up daisies – until they reached the deepest, oldest, dustiest one, with a creaky door marked:

The Flowers of Evil:
Madame Nanité, Underground Florist

Chapter Eight

They knocked politely, and walked in.

The room was lit by dozens of fluttering fireflies. Madame Vanité, who appeared to be half-human, half-mole, was sitting on a garden chair which hovered above the ground.

'This is a strange place to set up a florist's shop,' said Holly. 'Don't flowers need natural light?'

'Not these ones, my little pansy,' croaked Madame Vanité. 'They grow on dead bodies.'

'Oh great,' said Anna, 'at least if we can never get out of here again we know we'll be helping to grow your business.'

'You will get out of here again,' she said in her croaky voice. 'Or at least you'd better – it's your mission! Here's the wedding bouquet. Take it!'

She pointed at a perfectly plump, lovely-looking pink and white bouquet in a glass vase.

'Is that it?' Holly asked suspiciously. 'It looks normal to me.'

'It *is* normal, my little petunia,' said the florist, flashing two rows of black gums. 'Why wouldn't it be?'

Anna leaned forward and grabbed the bouquet.

Pepino covered his eyes: 'Ahhhh, I don't like this! I'm sure it's going to explode! Or worse, smell bad.'

'It's *fine*, Pepino,' Anna said. 'Let's go, before other skeletons find us.'

They ran out of the chamber and down the corridor they'd just taken.

At least, the one they *thought* they'd just taken.

'We came from the right, didn't we?' Holly asked.

'I think so,' said Anna, sounding very much unsure. They took another corridor full of hipbones. 'Left now, no?'

'Probably,' replied Holly. 'Sounds about right. I mean left. Right?'

'Right,' said Pepino. 'We go left.'

Left was an abandoned underground station in which sat a train full of skeletons.

'I don't remember this,' said Pepino.

'Maybe I wasn't paying attention. Where do we go from here?'

'It's all right,' said Anna. 'Let's go left. I mean right … Right?'

After an hour of aimless wandering, they had to admit the truth. 'We're *lost*, aren't we?' asked Pepino.

Anna nodded. 'I don't think we should have picked those flowers. We should have left them where they were.'

'But they looked so *pretty*!' Pepino cried. 'They just *begged* to be picked up! Oh *great*, just *great*, we're going to end up as skeletons too, now. And it's not as if you girls tried to make friends with the first ones we met!'

'Hey, *you*'re the one who switched their skulls around!' said Holly.

'Oh stop it. We're not going to be skeletons,' Anna said. 'We'll find our way out somehow. We just need to think.'

'I am thinking!' Pepino grumbled. 'I'm thinking I should be at home, eating ice cream in my pedal limousine. Instead we're here, all cold and wet and I've lost Charlotte A. Rainier.

And on top of that, something's scratching my neck!'

'It *is* Charlotte A. Rainier,' said Holly. 'She's on your shoulder.'

'Charlotte!' Pepino screamed. 'Hurrah! You're back!'

He kissed her on the cheek, so she bit him on the nose.

'*Ouch!*'

'Look,' Anna said, 'Charlotte's got a thread coming out of her belly and it leads all the way to …'

'To *where*?'

All the way back to the very first spiral staircase, where Charlotte A. Rainier had tied the tip of her thread to the bannister!

'Phew, Charlotte!' Holly said, stroking the spider's head. 'You saved our lives!'

The spider's eight eyes glowed with pride.

'That's the least she could do after biting me so much,' Pepino pointed out.

'Why, *bonsoir*,' said a cold, whispery voice behind them. 'I believe, warm-blooded humans, that you shouldn't be here. There's too much skin on those bones ...'

They turned around and faced the ghost

guardian, who was blocking the way out.

'Let us out of here,' Anna said. 'Or else …'

'Or else what?' the ghost said, breathing out a cloud of pure deathly coldness.

'My spider will bite you!' Pepino stated.

'She'd die on the spot,' the guardian replied.

'I'll kick you on the chin!' Anna warned.

She tried, but her foot went straight through the ghost's body, and she fell over on her bum.

'Wonderful,' said the ghost. 'I love it when I have a few warm humans to lock up down here and watch as they slowly turn into *skeletons*.'

He breathed out little puffs of gaseous deathliness.

'Wait a second,' said Holly. She plucked the bouquet from Anna's hand, and picked a flower from its core. 'You never see the light of day, Mr Ghost – what if I gave you a beautiful flower, smelling of sunlight and meadows, in exchange for our freedom?'

But as soon as he spotted the label on the wedding bouquet, the ghost shivered. 'Urgh! Don't – touch me with this!'

'Why not?'

'They aren't real flowers,' the ghost whispered. 'Madame Vanité only grows flowers of *evil*.'

'Oh really?' Holly smiled. 'You don't like them? Well, then – catch!'

She threw him the flower she'd squeezed out of the bouquet – and the ghost, looking horrified, collapsed through a stone wall and disappeared.

The three children scampered up the spiral staircase, and emerged into the canary-yellow morning sun.

'High five!' Pepino shouted, and managed

to high five Anna with three fingers out of five, which was an improvement on his previous attempts.

'High five, Holly!'

But Holly was in no mood to high five anyone. She looked disgusted.

She was staring at the bouquet from which one little flower had been plucked. And in the gap it had left, they could clearly see, coiled at the heart of the bouquet around the leaves and petals and thorns and little pink ribbons …

'Maggots!' Anna whispered. 'Well, well, well. Mademoiselle Malypense *really* wants to ruin that wedding, doesn't she?'

Chapter Nine

'*Merci!* How were the Catacombs?' Mademoiselle Malypense asked them, taking the bouquet from Holly's hands. 'Nice place, no?'

'A bit dark,' Anna said. 'And there was also the issue of, you know, skeletons. Unhappy ones.'

'Oh, did they bother you? I should have said – just a little kiss would have made it all right.

They're real softies, those skeletons. All they need is a bit of love.'

'Now you tell us,' Anna sighed, 'I had to beat them wearing a T-Rex's skull.'

'It was cool, though!' said Pepino.

'*Love*,' Holly mulled. 'That's a very powerful thing, isn't it, Mademoiselle Malypense?'

'It most certainly is,' mumbled the young lady, arranging the flowers near the wedding cake. 'Ready for your last mission?'

'Would you say that love is the *most powerful thing*, Mademoiselle?' Holly asked. 'Would you say it's bad to try to keep two people who love each other apart, if you love one of them?'

Mademoiselle Malypense froze. 'Why are you asking this?'

'Oh, nothing. Just wondering what you think about it. Would it be right?'

'W-w-well,' Mademoiselle Malypense stammered, but at that moment Kiki-Bisou growled furiously at the wedding bouquet. This seemed to shake Mademoiselle Malypense out of her reverie. 'Enough!' she said. 'Get to work. Your third mission starts *now!*'

'We haven't even had a *wink* of *sleep*,' Anna protested. 'We're exhausted!'

'You'll sleep tomorrow, even during the wedding ceremony if you like,' said Mademoiselle Malypense. 'Your services will not be required then.' And she trotted away, Kiki-Bisou yapping shrilly behind her.

As soon as she'd closed the door, however …

When they woke up, the sun was already halfway up the sky, and apparently enjoying the view after its morning climb.

'Right!' Anna said, stretching her arms and legs. 'Previous mission accomplished!'

She threw the Mission Plan on the floor, where it was destroyed by a colony of red ants, each one wearing a tiny balaclava.

'What's next?' Pepino asked. He was on top form after those few hours of sleep: he sprinted up one wall, then across half the ceiling, before falling into a large web that Charlotte A. Rainier had just had time to spin.

More ants crawled into the room carrying a rolled-up piece of paper tied with red ribbon. Holly picked it up and read out loud:

YOUR MISSION: PICKING UP THE WEDDING DRESS (WHITE ORGANZA, CREAM SILK AND IVORY SATIN)

WHERE: THE BELFRY OF THE
CATHEDRAL OF
NOTREDAM

WHEN: DURING THE DAY, WHEN THE
CATHEDRAL STAFF IS BUSY WITH ALL
THE TOURISTS. REMEMBER: STAY
DISCREET.
DON'T ATTRACT THE ATTENTION OF
TOURISTS.
GO ALL THE WAY UP THE SPIRAL
STAIRCASE IN THE LEFT TOWER.

'OH, NOT ANOTHER SPIRAL STAIRCASE!' Pepino complained.

'SHUSH! LET'S GO!' Anna shouted.

And they whooshed out of the palace without even bothering to open the door.

In front of the Cathedral of Notredam, Anna, Holly and Pepino had to climb over and under dozens of people who were asking their beloveds to marry them in all different languages:

'*Veux-tu m'épouser?*'

'*¿Te casarías conmigo?*'

'Ты выйдешь за меня?'

And some people had come from very far away to make their proposal.

Hundreds of people were trying to get into Notredam.

'Oh wow, so many Tourists,' said Pepino. 'It must mean this is a very boring monument.'

Holly and Anna had never seen Tourists before, so it was a bit of a shock.

'Zis way, please! Don't push!' shouted a severe-looking guardian at the door.

'Look! He's a *gargoyle*!' Pepino said.

'Don't point, it's rude,' said Holly. 'This way – we need to get to the left tower.'

In the left tower was a small wooden door which opened on to a narrow, dusty spiral staircase.

'When I'm King of Francia,' Pepino grumbled, 'I'll destroy all the spiral staircases in the country.'

'And replace them with what?' asked Holly.

'Trampolines, of course,' replied Pepino. 'One jump, and you'd already be at the top! Just like THAT! *OUCH!*'

Pepino had jumped a bit higher than planned, and bumped his head against a stone angel, who woke with a start.

'*Urghmp!* What's this? Is it the end of the world already?'

'Nope,' Anna said. 'It's nothing! You can fall asleep again.'

The angel yawned: 'Whoooo-h-h are you?'

'Just visitors. Come on!' Anna pressed Pepino and Holly onwards.

'This staircase leads to the belfry,' the angel said, peeling himself off the wall in a shower of stone dust. 'What are you doing there? Hey, wait!'

His granite wings were a bit stiff from all the

centuries of sleep, but he fluttered awkwardly behind Anna, Holly and Pepino. They hurried up the staircase, faster and faster and faster, until …

'*OUCH!*'

Pepino had kicked a small stone demon in the chin.

'Uh-oh …'

'*Pepino!*' Anna hissed. 'Can't you watch your step?'

'Sorry!' said Pepino. 'There wasn't a sign at the bottom of the staircase asking me to watch my step, you see, so I didn't. In Britland, there would *always* be a sign.'

'Quick, let's go …'

'*Aaaaaaah!!!!*' yawned the stone demon, spitting out a cloud of smoke and tiny lightning bolts. 'That was a good sleep! Is it the end of the world yet?'

'No,' said the stone angel, who'd caught up with them. 'I think those three humans are up to no good!'

'Up to no good? *GOOD!*' the demon bellowed. And he also detached himself from the wall, leaving chinks of stone everywhere on the steps.

'Oh *great*,' Anna sighed. 'We're being followed by an angel and a demon.'

Not only that, but behind them the angel and the demon bickered the whole way up to the top of the stairs. It was mostly incomprehensible:

'I won't let you let them be up to no good!'

piped the angel.

'I won't let you not let me let them be up to no good!' retorted the demon.

'I can't *believe* it,' said Anna to Pepino. 'Everywhere you go in this city you seem to wake up all the peacefully asleep monsters.'

'I also do that at home with my little brothers,' said Pepino sadly.

'This is it!' Holly whispered. 'What a strange place for a wedding dress to be made.'

The spiral staircase stopped at a little red door:

> ### Belles of the Belfry
> Made to measure fashionable outfits
> For all Notradamsels of all shapes and
> sizes. By appointment only if the damsel is
> a giantess, or a dragoness.

Knock, knock! went Holly's hand on the door.

'Come *iiiiin!*' went a singsong voice inside the room.

Chapter Ten

'Oh, I see,' Anna whispered next to Holly. 'It's not quite a … *normal* dressmaker.'

'*Normal?*' said a beautiful lady, greeting them at the door. 'Here, we're only concerned with what's *beautiful*. It doesn't matter if you've got two legs or ten, a nose or a beak; we find what suits you best. I'm Madame Esmeralda, by the way.'

The children shook hands with the lovely, graceful lady. The stone demon kissed Madame Esmeralda's hand, but the stone angel crossed his arms.

'This shop has no place in a cathedral! I will report you to the chief hunchback! Or even to God!'

'God? I made her a new dress last week, so I don't believe she minds,' said Madame Esmeralda. 'Come along, my dears, we'll show you the Royal Wedding Dress. I'm sure you'll agree it's simply gorgeous.'

'What do you *mean*,' asked the stone angel, 'by "the Royal Wedding Dress"? Surely *you* weren't asked to design such a dress? Or did this country become ruled by *monsters* while I was asleep?'

'Princess Violette,' said Madame Esmeralda, 'requires the most exquisite wedding dress Francia can offer, and her wedding organiser thought that I was the best dressmaker for the task.'

They circled around the huge dress draped on the bell. 'Who's that one for, Madame Esmeralda?' Holly asked, transfixed.

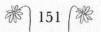

'The biggest belle of Notredam,' replied the designer. 'But yours is right *here* – I'm sure you can guess which one.'

'It's *beautiful*!' said Holly. 'And very normal-looking! Erm, I mean, *human*-looking.'

Madame Esmeralda unpinned it from the mannequin and folded it into a box, which she tied carefully with a thick white ribbon. 'Here we are, my darlings … I'll let you get on, now – I can see Mademoiselle Médusa over there coming to try on her wedding dress. Bye-bye!'

Mademoiselle Médusa, who'd just walked in, was a funny sort of fiancée.

'Oh, the *evil creature*!' the angel moaned. 'She'll turn you all to stone with her eyes!'

'Shush!' said Madame Esmeralda. 'You are *so* rude! Besides, she's wearing safety goggles. Now, goodbye!'

And she sauntered away to attend to Mademoiselle Médusa.

Anna grabbed the box with the dress. 'Well, that was easy!'

'*Too* easy,' the angel hissed. 'What exactly is going on here? You three are acting *very* suspiciously. And I can smell *evil* in that box.'

'They're just doing their job, Ange,' smirked the demon. 'And doing it very well indeed. *Everything* will be *perfectly* ruined.'

He tapped Holly's shoulder in approval.

'What do you mean, *everything*?' Holly asked.

'He means,' the angel said, 'that because of you three, something *very* sinful will happen!'

'What does *sinful* mean?' asked Pepino.

'Evil!' the angel said. 'Horrible! Awful! Devilish!'

'Like a global shortage of ice cream?'

The angel looked a bit perplexed. 'Erm, no. Not like that at all.'

'Oh, then it's OK,' Pepino declared. 'Let's go.'

But Holly was in two minds.

'What if the angel's right?' she asked. 'What if we're doing something really *evil*?'

'Evil is *good*!' the demon snorted. 'Do it!'

'Come on, Holly,' Anna replied. 'We're just doing this to earn money. It's not our fault if Mademoiselle Malypense is up to something wicked.'

'It is!' the angel cried. 'You will be making *dirty* money!'

'It isn't!' the demon chuckled. 'You will be having a lot of *fun* with that money!'

'Oh, this is so confusing!' Holly whispered.

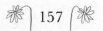

'Anna, I don't think we should –'

'Come *on*!' Anna groaned. She grabbed her sister by the hand, but Holly refused to budge.

'Don't go, Holly,' the angel murmured. 'Your sister is wrong. You're right. She's younger.

You're older and wiser. She's just trying to get you into trouble.'

'Just do it,' the demon added. 'You'll have fun, both of you, spending all that easy money … After all, that's what you want, don't you? Having fun with her, your darling sister …'

'*Enough!*' Anna shouted. 'I'm going to turn you both back to stone, as you deserve! MADEMOISELLE MEDUSA! LOOK HERE!'

Mademoiselle Médusa looked at the angel.

PFSHAK! The angel froze, and fell on the floor.

Mademoiselle Médusa looked at the demon.

PFSHAK! The demon froze, and fell on the floor.

'Thank you,' Anna said, 'that was very helpful of …'

But before she put her safety goggles back on, Mademoiselle Médusa couldn't help but look at Holly, who was standing right between angel and demon.

PFSHAK!

Holly froze.

And fell on the floor.

BAM.

'Oh, Anna,' said Pepino. 'That's not a nice way of making your sister shut up. Even *I* wouldn't do that to my brothers, and they're much more annoying than she is.'

For a moment it looked like Anna had frozen, too.

'I'm *so sorry*,' Mademoiselle Médusa said, putting on her goggles. She trotted towards them

on her high heels. 'But it was careless of you, calling me like that when I was just swapping goggles!'

'*Sossorry! Sossorry! Sossorry!*' hissed the snakes on her head.

Anna had dropped to her knees and was slapping Holly's cheeks.

'Wow!' Pepino said. 'You *really* must *hate* her! Isn't it enough that she's a statue now? You have to *slap* her too?'

'I'm trying to wake her up, you dunce! How do I wake her up?' Anna asked Médusa. 'How? *How?*'

'I'm sorry, my dear,' said Madame Esmeralda, 'It is quite impossible to revive people who have been petrified. I'm afraid she'll stay like that forever.'

'Ha-ha! *Forever*.' Pepino laughed. 'When my parents say, "you're grounded forever!", I know it just means, "for ten minutes", because then they get bored and ask me back to play IT with them.'

'That's not the same *forever* as *this* forever,' Mademoiselle Médusa said. 'This forever is a *forever* forever. So sorry.'

'*Sossorry! Sossory! Sossorry!*' susurrated the snakes.

And just then Pepino noticed Anna's eyes were all wet, as if it *really* was a *forever forever*

sort of forever.

'Oh, ANNA!' he bawled. 'How COULD YOU do this to Holly? She's by FAR my favourite of the two of you!'

They couldn't cry for long, however, because the biggest belle of Notredam had just landed on the edge of the huge west-facing belfry window.

She was a mahoosive, ginormous, megasized dragoness, and she looked very impatient to try on her wedding dress.

Chapter Eleven

'Oh, Miss Crackamatch!' Madame Esmeralda exclaimed. 'You *know* you're not supposed to come here during the day! *Everyone* will have seen you!'

Anna and Pepino ran to the window and looked down. Indeed, all the Tourists' heads were pointing towards the belfry, taking hundreds of pictures, and cries could be heard

in many different languages: 'Dragon! Dragon! Dragon!'

The dragoness pointed at the dress wrapped around the huge bell, and grunted. A puff of flames burnt a nearby hatstand, which was reduced to ashes.

'*Yes*,' Madame Esmeralda said, 'you'll get to try it on – but it's *by appointment only*! Oh, dear, oh dear – Monsieur Gargouille will be up here in no time to tell me off!'

She turned to Anna and Pepino. 'You must leave now. Monsieur Gargouille is the Chief

Gargoyle Guardian of Notredam. He doesn't
– erm – exactly *know* about the Royal Wedding
Dress being made here. If he finds you here,
Mademoiselle Malypense will be in big trouble.
Go!'

'I can't leave my sister,' Anna said. She tried to
lift Holly, but she was too heavy.

Pepino dragged Holly by her plaits, but they
both broke. 'Oh, whoops! She's going to be upset
when she wakes up and finds she's had a hair
cut.'

'Don't worry, my love, she'll never wake up,'

Madame Esmeralda said. 'Miss Crackamatch, you must leave immediately. Please take these children with you – as well as their statue. Off you fly! Off you fly!'

Looking furious, the dragoness picked up Holly in her front claws, and Anna and Pepino jumped on her back. They were only just in time – the door flew open, and the gargoyle guardian they'd seen downstairs rushed in.

'Madame Esmeralda! What is *this* about? It's already nice of us to *tolerate* you and your demonic tailoring shop in this holy place, but we've told you – you can't have that kind of clientele during the day!'

The dragoness was visibly unhappy to be called 'that kind of clientele'. In one huff, she burnt down one of the ropes on which the huge bell hung.

The bell swung to one side, emitting the loudest *DONG! DONG! DONG!* Anna and Pepino had ever heard.

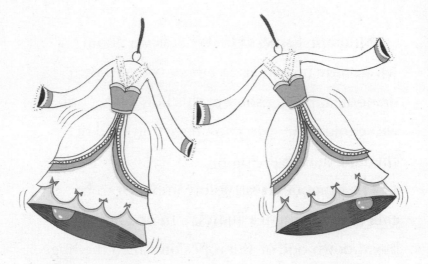

'Is it breakfast time already?' the statues
of saints on the walls of Notredam asked one
another, waking up from their daily sleep and
creeping out of their little alcoves.

'NO! No, it's NOT!'
Monsieur Gargouille
vociferated. 'Go back to
sleep! And who are those
humans she's carrying on
her back? GARGOYLE
PATROL! CATCH THAT
DRAGONESS!'

The dragoness swiftly leapt out of the
window. A dozen gargoyles wrenched themselves
from the walls and they flapped their stone wings
to reach the dragoness.

FLASH! FLASH! FLASH!
went the Tourists' eyes below.
FROOOOOOOOSH! The
dragoness spat a huge cloud of
fire on the gargoyle patrol. But they were made
of stone, not wood – so instead of burning, they
continued to attack …

SMACK!

Anna kicked a monkey-
faced, lizard-bodied
gargoyle in the chest. He
crashed against the wall

of Notredam.

POW!

Pepino punched a goat-
faced, dog-bodied gargoyle on the snout. She
whirled down and caught her breath on a little
stone balcony.

PAF!

Anna slapped a dishevelled, lion-like
gargoyle with the box that
contained the dress.
The box was wrenched
open, and the dress flew

from Anna's grasp . . .

'NO!'

Then the dress did something very peculiar.
It fluttered around for a bit … and then flew *back
towards them*!

'How is that *possible*?' Anna mused, grabbing
on to the dress and folding it up again. 'Oh …
I see …'

What she'd seen, tucked under the lining of the dress, was a vast colony of bats.

'Another one of Mademoiselle Malypense's tricks,' Anna mumbled. 'I bet this dress is full of them. How ridiculous! Miss Crackamatch,' she said to the dragoness. 'Please, will you take us back to the Royal Palace? Can you fly there?'

The dragoness nodded, munched a last small, shrieking pig-like gargoyle to dust, and then dodged a flock of eagle-bodied, snake-faced gargoyles.

'Go, go, go!' Anna shouted. 'Please!'

The dragoness whooshed up above the belfry in the left tower – then curved down towards the right tower, but the gargoyles weren't giving up that easily.

SWISH! She was gone again, straight down on to the crowd of Tourists. (*AAAAHHHHH!!!!*) And towards the river, heading straight for the nearest bridge …

At the last second, she pulled up, leaving the gargoyles to crash miserably against the bridge. *SPLOSH SPLOSH SPLOSH SPLOSH!*

The blocks of stone tumbled down into the

dark green river.

DONG! DONG! DONG!

The big bell inside Notredam was still ringing
– and continued to ring for hours.

It was still ringing after the dragoness had
dropped off Anna and Pepino at the Royal
Palace.

And after they'd given Mademoiselle
Malypense the box with the dress.

And even after Mademoiselle Malypense had
confirmed to them, looking at Holly's stone face:

'The poor child. There's nothing to be done,

I'm afraid. When people are turned to stone, it's *forever*.'

DONG! DONG! DONG!

The bell rang all night. And neither Pepino nor Anna managed to sleep.

Chapter Twelve

The next morning was the Royal Wedding Day, but Anna and Pepino weren't in the mood for a party.

'It's not even going to *be* a party anyway,' Anna moaned. 'The wedding cake has garlic in it, the wedding bouquet has a crowd of creepy-crawlies in it, and the wedding dress has bats in it. All so that Mademoiselle Malypense can get

King Dentu to call off his wedding to Princess Violette. It's absurd!'

'Time to go, children,' said Mademoiselle Malypense, walking into their room. 'Your last mission, should you wish to be paid, is to help me carry all this stuff to the ceremony, at the Palace of Versaï. It's a short carriage ride out of Parii. Princess Violette has been staying there this past month with her parents and sister.'

'Why is the wedding not taking place in Parii?' Anna asked.

'Better to be as far away from Pariisians as

possible,' said Mademoiselle Malypense. 'They'd ruin the ceremony.'

'I see. And you *wouldn't* want the ceremony to be ruined, would you?' smirked Anna.

'Of course not. Get ready!'

They piled up the wedding cake, the baguettes, the dress and the bouquet at the back of a royal carriage drawn by six giant roosters: two blue, two white, two red. They also laid down Holly's stone body on the back seat.

'*COCORICO!*' the roosters all screamed in unison.

'That's *cock-a-doodle-doo* in Francian,' said Mademoiselle Malypense. 'That means they're ready. Let's go!'

The roosters flapped their wings, clicked their claws, and began to pull the carriage down the streets. There were as many police officers on rhinoceros-back in the city as there were Pariisians.

'They don't look too happy that their princess is getting married,' Pepino observed.

SPLOSH! A very smelly egg crashed on the carriage near Mademoiselle Malypense's face.

'SAY *NON* TO ROYALTY!' someone screamed in the crowd.

'*NON!*' the crowd said. '*NON AUX PRINCESSES! NON AUX PRINCES! NON AUX ROIS ! NON AUX REINES!*'

'What are they saying?' asked Pepino.

'No to princesses, no to princes,

no to kings, no to queens,' Mademoiselle
Malypense translated calmly. 'The usual stuff.'

'Oh,' said Pepino, trying to make
himself as small as possible. 'Perhaps
I won't invade Francia after all.'

SMACK! Another egg crashed
against the carriage.

'Hey,' said Anna, 'that was an
ostrich's egg! That's *dangerous*!'

'And it smells ten times more rotten!' Pepino
added. 'Yuck!'

Mademoiselle Malypense clicked her tongue,

and the roosters sped up a bit, but not fast enough to her taste. She got out a baguette, snapped it open, and placed a large chunk into a slingshot.

POP!

The chunk of bread flew into the air and landed a long way down the avenue. The roosters sped towards the bread and pecked it down.

Mademoiselle Malypense armed the slingshot with another chunk of bread …

'OUTRAGE!' screamed the crowd.

'*SCANDALE!*'

'What's their problem *now*?' Anna asked as the roosters sped to the next bit of bread.

'They say I'm wasting bread on an expensive trip to Versaï for a Royal Wedding that won't bring anything to the country. Oh, and that life is unfair and meaningless,' explained Mademoiselle Malypense.

And she casually flung a third chunk of bread further down the avenue.

The rhinoceros police could no longer contain the angry crowd.

Pariisians poured in from all sides, running furiously towards the carriage. The roosters pressed on, their glassy black eyes unreadable, but their shivering feathers betrayed the fact that something was about to happen …

The next time Anna looked, the carriage was twenty metres above the ground!

'They can *fly*?' stammered Anna, holding

on to Pepino, who was holding on to Kiki-
Bisou, who was holding on to Mademoiselle
Malypense.

'Very badly, as you can tell,' snapped
Mademoiselle Malypense.

And indeed it was the rockiest, clumsiest,
most awkward flight Anna and Pepino had ever

been on. The roosters were terrible at flying –
sometimes one of them would lurch, throwing
the whole carriage on its side, and then another
few would go up while others went down …

'I'm going to be sick,' Pepino warned.

'Not on my dress!' shouted Mademoiselle
Malypense.

So he was sick on Anna instead. 'Uh-oh,' he
said as he sat up, 'there's this weird kind of tower
coming our way …'

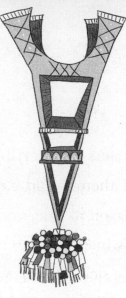

'Of course it's not coming our way,'
Mademoiselle Malypense mumbled. '*We're*
headed straight for it. It's –'

CLANG!

Everyone was holding on tight as the carriage
hit the tower, apart from ...

'HOLLY!' yelled Anna.

Holly's statue was hanging from a metal beam by one arm, and getting smaller and smaller as the carriage moved off into the distance …

'I'll get her!' Pepino screamed. 'Charlotte, quick – some thread!'

And holding Charlotte's web in his hands – he *jumped*!

'Please don't let me down, Charlotte A. Rainier – please don't let me down …'

Charlotte A. Rainier was certainly *not* going to let Pepino down.

Pepino landed
on the iron beam,
and wrapped his
free arm around
Holly's waist. A few
seconds later, the
thread tightened,
and they were
hurled into the sky,
behind the carriage
drawn by the six
frantic roosters.

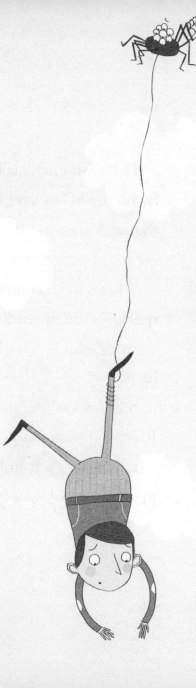

'This isn't fair,' said Pepino. 'The one time I risk my life to save her, and she hasn't even noticed.'

Chapter Thirteen

They got to Versaï ten minutes before the wedding ceremony.

'Here you are!' Princess Violette cried as Mademoiselle Malypense opened the door to her apartments. 'I thought you'd had an accident, or – or that you'd decided not to come!'

Pepino, Anna and even Mademoiselle Malypense and Kiki-Bisou were a bit stunned

by the sudden appearance of Princess Violette –
who really was quite a beautiful young lady.

'No, no, we were simply delayed,'
Mademoiselle Malypense stammered. 'But we
have everything we need, Violette – everything.'

'Are you sure?'

'Oh yes,' whispered Mademoiselle Malypense. 'It will all be well in the end.' She coughed, and turned around to look at Anna and Pepino. 'You two – go sit in the Gallery of Mirrors. That's where the ceremony will take place. I must do Violette's make-up … not that you *need* any, of course …'

Pepino and Anna tumbled down the stairs. The Gallery of Mirrors didn't have any mirrors in it; or if it did, they'd been covered by strange black curtains. The ceiling, however, was richly

painted and gilded. Someone had installed the Royal Wedding Cake at the front of the room, and Holly's stone statue was standing near the first row.

The room was full of royalty from all different countries:

The Royal Family of Francia, of course: King Louis the Eighty-Ninth, Queen Marianne, and Princess Violette's younger sister, Princess Bella.

The Emir of Antarktik,
who'd come with his
bodyguard.

The Sultana of Californy,
who'd surfed all the way to
Francia.

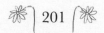

The Empress and
Emperor of Swedenorway,
extremely happy, as always,
with all their extremely
successful children
… and also …

'Mummy! Daddy!'

'Oh, hello, Pepino
darling,' said the Queen
of Britland. 'Where's
your crown? You look so

silly without it. We were wondering where you'd gone!'

'The boat sent a message in Morse code to the Royal Castle when we left,' said Anna. 'To say where we were going and for how long, and to tell you to tell my mother about it, too. Didn't you get the message?'

'Oh!' exclaimed the King, tapping his head. 'Was it something like – *beep beep! Bip bip beeeeep! Bip bip?*'

'Probably.'

'Well, we don't know Morse code. Send actual words next time.'

'You mean my mum doesn't know where we are?' Anna gasped. 'She must be worried sick!'

'Is your mum the bothersome woman who's been coming to the Royal Castle, crying a lot, repeating that she's lost her two daughters, and asking us if we know where they are?'

'*Yes*,' Anna hiccoughed, 'that would be her! Oh, dear! She must be so upset. And now Holly's been turned to stone ...'

'Shush!' said the Queen. 'The ceremony is starting.'

The little seraphs and goddesses in the painted ceiling had begun to play a rather gloomy piece of music. Everyone turned around. King Dentu and Princess Violette were slowly walking down the aisle. Waiting for them at the end of the aisle was a grumpy-looking little Cupid, who had been hired to perform the ceremony.

'What a happy couple they make!' King Steve whispered, squashing a tear on his cheek.

When they reached the front of the room, Mademoiselle Malypense dropped Princess Violette's long trail to the floor, nudged King Dentu a bit towards the Royal Cake, and sat down on a chair in the front row.

'Welcome, All Your Majesties,' said the Cupid in a high-pitched voice. He shuffled through his registry. 'We are here today to witness the marriage of the most excellent King Bram Dentu of Romany, with the Francian princess and heiress to the throne, Violette Eugénie Marie Calliste ...'

He began to read out Princess Violette's twenty-eight other middle names. Everyone waited patiently.

Everyone except King Dentu.

'Colette …'

'Simone …'

'Françoise …'

'Delphine …'

Mademoiselle Malypense interrupted the reading, whispering very audibly, 'Are you quite all right, Your Majesty?'

'The cake,' King Dentu croaked. 'Must we – erm – have it here in the room?'

'But of course,' said Mademoiselle Malypense. 'It is tradition to serve it immediately after the ceremony!'

The Cupid started reading again. 'Solange …'

King Dentu was getting paler and paler by the minute. 'This cake!' he finally erupted. 'It smells of *garlic*!'

Pepino nudged Anna. 'Told you he wouldn't like it! He's a man of taste.'

'King Dentu, *please!*' said Mademoiselle Malypense. 'It's a Francian delicacy. If you really can't bear the smell, ask your fiancée to lend you her bouquet of flowers for the duration of the ceremony.'

Princess Violette passed the groom her bouquet of flowers, and King Dentu buried his nose in it. 'King Dentu!' said the Cupid. 'Do you take Princess Violette to be your lawful wedded wife?'

Mademoiselle Malypense sat up on her chair, visibly tense. Anna whispered to Pepino: 'She's hoping he'll say no! She's hoping he'll say he'll marry her instead!'

King Dentu lifted his face off the flowers to reply.

Princess Violette looked at him – and screamed – and fainted!

'What is this?' King Louis the Eighty-Ninth

exclaimed. 'Maggots! Cockroaches! Flies! Who put all these creepy-crawlies in the wedding bouquet?'

'And more importantly,' Queen Marianne piped, 'why are they *eating* King Dentu's *face*?'

King Dentu furiously wiped his face. 'Let's carry on with the ceremony!' he roared.

'Just a minute, Your Majesty,' said Mademoiselle Malypense. 'I'm trying to revive your bride.'

Mademoiselle Malypense lifted the princess's feet up on to a chair, sending dozens of bats flying around the room …

Which all gathered around King Dentu!

'Why, bats seem to like you a *lot*, Your Majesty!' said Mademoiselle Malypense. She turned to the audience. 'Isn't it strange, Your Other Majesties? King Dentu hates the smell of garlic. His face is very attractive to maggots. And bats naturally fly towards him! What could that *mean*?'

The Royal Guests pondered the answer. For two minutes.

Three minutes.

Ten minutes.

Scratching their heads and beards.

215

Until Anna finally yawned and said, 'I don't mean to be rude to royalty, but the ones in this room aren't the brightest light bulbs. Let me guess. Maybe, just maybe – he's a *vampire*?'

The word unleashed a torrent of cries and whispers in the audience. 'A VAMPIRE!'

'Yes!' said Mademoiselle Malypense. 'A VAMPIRE! Such is the man King Louis the Eighty-Ninth wants to give his daughter to! A vampire, who would have bitten our Princess the moment they were pronounced man and wife! Kiki-Bisou – pull the rope!'

Kiki-Bisou yapped, jumped up, and grabbed a cord between his teeth. The black curtains around the room fell down, revealing dozens of gleaming mirrors.

None of them reflected King Dentu!

King Dentu's frown was deeper than the Catacombs. 'I don't care!' he bellowed. 'I *will* have Princess Violette's blood, whether I'm married to her or not!'

And he made a run for Princess Violette's neck!

BLING!

'Sorry, Your Majesty,' said Mademoiselle Malypense. 'I had the collar reinforced with solid silver. Did it hurt your teeth?'

'Fif if a FCANDAL!' yelled King Dentu. 'I'm LEAVING FIS PLAFE!'

Princess Bella, Princess Violette's younger sister, rushed to the front. 'Oh please, King Dentu!' she cried. 'Takc me instead! I love vampires!'

King Dentu looked at her, shrugged, and nodded. He took her by the hand, and jumped up – two large bat wings opened behind his back – and they smashed through the window and

disappeared into the blue sky.

'Well, that was entertaining,' said Pepino. 'Mademoiselle Malypense did ruin this wedding in the end. But I don't understand. I thought she was in love with King Dentu.'

Anna smiled at him. 'I think, maybe, it wasn't quite what we thought, Pepino …'

'Oh, Jeanne!' said Princess Violette to Mademoiselle Malypense. 'You saved me from this horrible man!'

'I couldn't have let him marry you, Violette. We've known one another since we were little girls – I knew you couldn't be happy with him.'

'Oh, Jeanne – what would I do without you? I don't think I ever want to marry anyone. I'd much rather stay with you and play in the Royal Gardens forever.'

Queen Marianne huffed and puffed. 'You are twenty-five years old, my dear. It *is* time to put away childish things and get married.'

'Is it, Mother?' Violette asked defiantly. 'Well, then – Jeanne, my dearest friend – will you marry me?'

Mademoiselle Malypense's already-quite-

large-eyes widened even more. 'Well, I – I – of course I will!'

'And I will marry you!' declared Princess Violette.

'What do you mean, marry *her*?' bellowed King Louis the Eighty-Ninth. 'She's not even royalty!'

Princess Violette frowned a lovely frown. 'Oh, Daddy,' she said, 'don't be so old-fashioned! Everywhere in the world my prince and princess friends are marrying total peasants. Dear friends, I take Jeanne Malypense to be my lawful wedded wife.'

'And I,' said Mademoiselle Malypense, 'take Princess Violette of Francia to be my lawful wedded wife, too.'

The fluttering Cupid was wildly jotting down notes on the registry, looking extremely annoyed at the disruption. 'Well, just a minute, let me scratch out the previous name! All right, all right – I declare you wife and wife, then.'

'*WAF 'N' WAF!*' yapped Kiki-Bisou.

Everyone clapped very loudly, and both brides blushed beautifully.

And then Princess Violette and Madame

Malypense left in their honeybee-drawn carriage, to go on honeymoon to the moon.

'Well,' said Pepino, 'that was a nice happy ever after. I don't even mind that Mademoiselle Malypense seems to have forgotten to pay us.'

Anna shrugged. 'Why would we want to get paid anyway? Now that Holly's a statue forever, it wouldn't be any fun going on a Holy Moly Holiday.'

Chapter Fourteen

Back in Doverport, their little seaside village in the south of Britland, Anna had to explain to her mum why they'd gone to Parii without telling her, and why Holly was now useful only as a garden decoration.

'My poor little Holly!' Mrs Burnbright cried. 'I wept buckets of tears when you were away, and now there are many more to come! Look, they're here, in the garden. I figured I might as well keep them to water the plants …'

She'd indeed hung quite a large quantity of buckets from the complicated branches of a gnarly tree. Pepino stood up to look at them. 'Wow!' he said. 'That's a lot of tears. I don't think I've ever cried so much, even when I grazed my ankle falling off my gold-plated skateboard …'

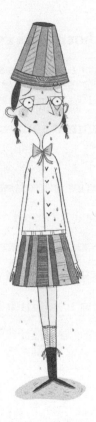

'Pepino, careful!'
Anna exclaimed. 'You're
pushing the buckets
towards …'

CRASSSHHHH!!
and *SPLOSSSHHHH!*

'Oh no,' said Mrs
Burnbright. 'Now I can't
even water my plants
with them!'

Cough! Cough!

'What's this, Anna?

Why are you coughing? You're not catching a
cold, are you?'

Cough, cough, cough!

'It's not me!' Anna cried. 'Mummy! It's …
It's …'

'HOLLY!!!!'

'Magic mummy tears,' said Mrs Burnbright. 'I should have known! I can't believe old-fashioned tricks like that still work.'

'Oh, Holly!' Anna wailed. 'I'm so sorry I made Mademoiselle Médusa turn you to stone!'

'And I'm so sorry I accidentally broke your plaits,' said Pepino. 'But you look great with short hair, too!'

'And I'm *so sorry* I kept going on about the Holy Moly Holiday,' said Anna. 'We don't need to go anywhere. We're perfectly happy here! We can just stay around and lie on the beach and do nothing at all for the rest of the summer.'

Holly coughed out some more magic mummy tears. 'Certainly not!' she said. 'I've been stone cold for much too long. I need action! I need adventure! I need …'

She jumped up and down a bit to get the blood running back into her veins …

'I NEED A HOLY MOLY HOLIDAY!'

'OK,' said Pepino, 'but we still haven't got any money.'

'Well, in that case,' said Holly, 'I guess we'll need to find another job …'